When Dog Was Little

by LUCILLE HAMMOND
illustrated by EUGENIE

A GOLDEN BOOK · NEW YORK
Western Publishing Company, Inc., Racine, Wisconsin 53404

THIS is Dog.
   Dog is big enough to go to nursery school. He is big enough to have a teacher and to be with other dogs.

But once upon a time, before he went to school, Dog was not big. He was little. He was so little that he drank his milk from a bottle.

When he ate his lunch, he sat in a high chair and his mother fed him with a spoon.

Because he was so little,
Dog slept in a crib.

When Dog was little he used to cry
a lot. He cried when he was hungry...

...and he cried when his mother and father had to go out.

Sometimes Dog would cry for no reason at all! Then his mother would pick him up and give him a hug.

Or she would rock him in her arms and sing him a song. That made Dog feel better, and most of the time he would stop crying.

Before long Dog had some teeth. Then he could eat grown-up food. He could eat apples and carrots and toast.

And Dog began to crawl. Soon he could move all around the room.

Dog learned to talk, and then he could tell his mother what he liked to do.

He could also tell his mother what
he did *not* like to do!

Most of the time Dog played with his own toys. But sometimes he liked to play with his mother's or father's things, especially if they were hard to reach.

Then his mother or his father would get cross and say, "No, no, Dog. That is not for you!"

Dog learned to walk, and then to run.
His mother often said, "That Dog runs
so fast I can hardly catch him!"

One day in the park Dog's mother stopped
to talk but Dog kept on running. When his
mother tried to find him, he was gone.

"Help! Help!" Dog's mother cried. "I've lost
my little dog!"

But Dog was not really lost. He was just watching some other dogs playing on the slide.

Not long after that Dog learned how to dress and undress himself. He could button his own buttons and take off his shoes and socks.

And finally Dog was big enough to have a new bed. He said good-bye to his crib and hello to a big bed just the right size for big dogs.

Dog is glad that he is big. He can hardly believe that once upon a time he was little.

Good night, Dog.